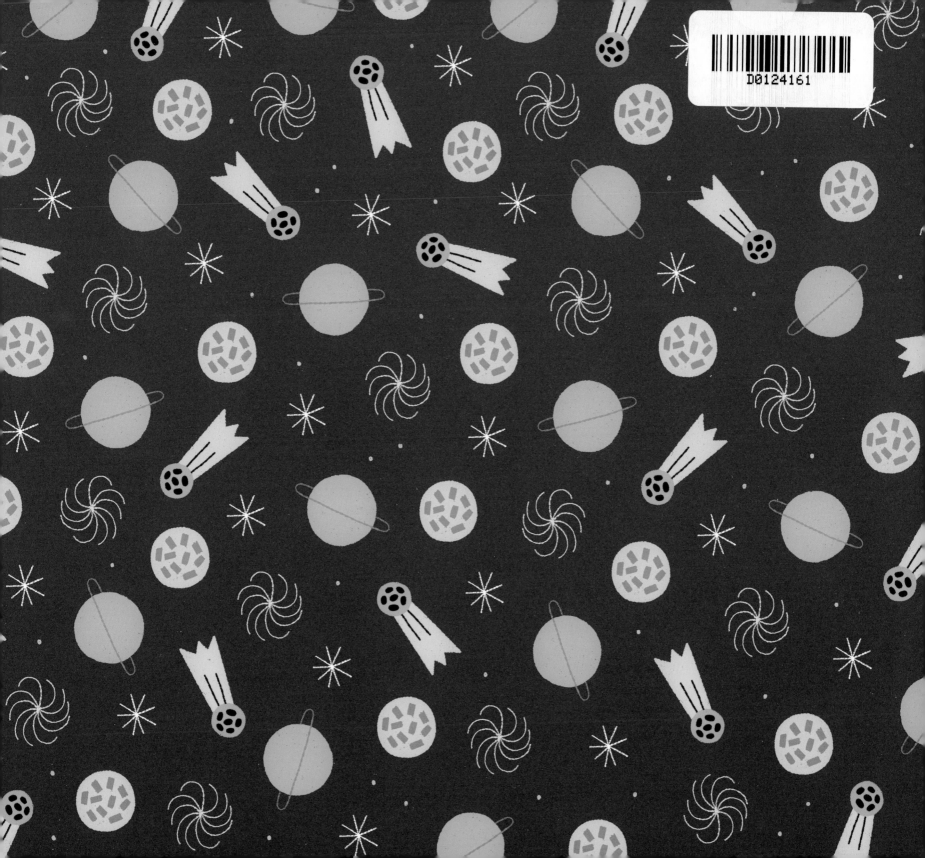

D0124161

YAAAAAAWN! *Night night!*

And now that it is bedtime,
the yawn has come for YOU!

It started with a **yawn**
that grew **and** grew **and** grew.

YAAAAAAWN!
Pass it on!

Do your eyes feel heavy?
Are...you...yawning...yet?

This little yawn has traveled.
You're feeling tired, I bet....

YAAAAAAAWN! *Pass it on!*

Aliens from **outer space** will all be yawning soon.

It snuck aboard a **rocket**, and it's heading for the **Moon!**

YAAAAAAAWN! Pass it on!

To **elephants** in scorching sun, the yawn is on the go!

From **polar bears** to **penguins** in freezing ice and snow...

YAAAAAAAWN!
Pass it on!

YAWNING ST.

On high speed trains and buses —
the yawn is **everywhere!**

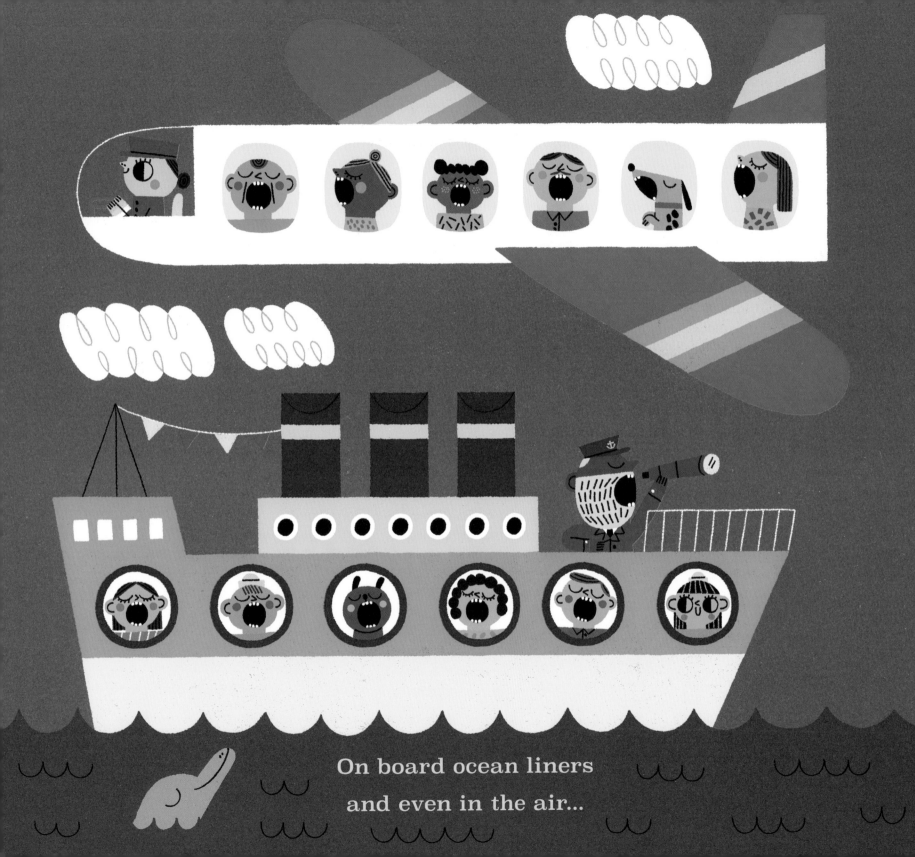

On board ocean liners
and even in the air...

A yawn can be **persistent** —

it's **useless** to resist!

The yawn is **rumbling** around the world —

no person will be **missed**.

YAAAAAAWN!

Pass it on!

This yawn will not be happy
until **everyone's** asleep!

Spreading through the countryside,
the yawn hits **cows** and **sheep**.

YAAAAAWN!

Pass it on!

PLANTS

WELCOME

I bet you're yawning, too!

The **cat** is feeling sleepy —
she slinks inside the house.

Be **careful!** Oh, no! There it goes!
He passed it to the **cat!**

Now the **dog** is yawning —
what do you think of that?

I don't know where it came from —

somewhere deep inside?

I just can't seem to stop it,

even though I've tried.

YAWN!
Pass it on!

It started with a

that came out of the **blue**.

You know you just can't help it —
you'll soon be **yawning**, too!

YAWN

Fountaindale Public Library District
300 W. Briarcliff Rd.
Bolingbrook, IL 60440

by
Patricia Hegarty

tiger tales

Illustrated by
Teresa Bellón

For Jake
P.H.

To my beloved parents,
Sebastián and Teresa
T.B.

tiger tales

5 River Road, Suite 128, Wilton, CT 06897
Published in the United States 2021
Originally published in Great Britain 2020
by Caterpillar Books Ltd.
Text by Patricia Hegarty
Text copyright © 2020 Caterpillar Books Ltd.
Illustrations copyright © 2020 Teresa Bellón
ISBN-13: 978-1-68010-234-5
ISBN-10: 1-68010-234-6
Printed in China
CPB/1800/1610/1020
All rights reserved
2 4 6 8 10 9 7 5 3 1

www.tigertalesbooks.com

W9-BLI-461